ALONG THE RIVER'S EDGE

Kit Shaw

PART ONE

THE SOUL

CHAPTER ONE

When I opened my eyes, all I saw was the never-ending sky.

Fluffy white cotton across an expanse of saturated blue.

It would've been peaceful and pleasant if not for the impending panic squeezing my chest.

I was dying.

I gasped, sucking in air like I hadn't taken a breath in years. My arms reflexively began to flail, disturbing the water I was just becoming aware of around me. Finally, the sound hit me. The crashing of water, my muffled and garbled gasping and wailing as I fought against the current.

It was like my senses were slowly returning.

I was coming back together piece by piece, and it was a torturous process.

Water was slipping into my mouth and being sucked into my lungs, burning my throat and chest only to then burn my nose as everything suddenly rushed back up and out of me. I retched as my legs finally found the muddy floor beneath me. Embarrassingly, I was only in around a foot of water, but it might as well have been the depth of the ocean.

I rooted myself into the loose earth and clawed myself up and onto my knees.

Hot and acidic fluid poured from my mouth and my nose, choking me and forcing my eyes shut. My entire body was shaking uncontrollably, and hot tears were slipping from between my eyelids and sliding down my face. Who knows how long I retched and cried, choking up all of the water I had swallowed, but by the time I opened my eyes and steadied my breathing, the bright blue sky I had seen before was aglow with orange and pink.

My chest heaved as I breathed, taking in my surroundings.

I was in a thin river, the bank covered in rocks and pebbles forming miniature mountain edges. Along either side was an imposing forest, with trees that had such thick trunks that the spaces between were choked and suffocated with the encroaching underbrush. They were also quite tall, forming canopies that cast deep shadows across the ground, nearing the water's edge.

I had no recollection of where this was or how I got here.

More terrifying, I didn't know who I was.

I was thankful I was alive, but otherwise, I felt an intense emptiness that was steadily being filled with terror over the unknown.

I stared down the length of the river, which seemed to go on forever until it took a sharp turn and disappeared behind more trees. But it was right as the river began to curve that I caught sight of something out of place in the sense that it was sentient. Like me, it was moving and alive.

There was a man crouched along the river's edge. His eyes were bright gold, and his hair was so light that I couldn't discern whether it was white or blond, but it was thin and wispy, like feathers sprouting from his head. But more eye-catching than that was the set of antlers growing from his head.

They were glowing with a white haze that seemed to emanate from within them. He reminded me of a deer as he stared in my direction, light eyes wide and bulging as he froze.

His mouth opened like he might say something, only to close as he swallowed in complete silence, still staring. As he stood, his body was covered in a thick and heavy cloak that enveloped his form entirely. Its great folds fell to the ground, kicking up a fine cloud of dust, but the inky black fabric remained untouched.

It was only when he began to move, stepping along the shore of the river, that his form became more apparent. With each step, he kicked the bottom of the cloak aside. From within, a hoofed foot strode outward, hitting the stony earth with a satisfying clack. It was cloven, much like I would expect from a deer, attached to a tawny fur-covered leg.

Awestruck, I was frozen, unable to react as this man — no, this *being* — moved closer and closer to me.

As he neared, a powerful, warming aura emanated from his person. It was intense yet comfortable, enough to soften my muscles and leave me lying casually in the river. I might have fallen asleep if not for the man's eyes, which had me fully entranced.

"You aren't supposed to be here."

I blinked.

"Yeah."

He tilted his head, a slight twitch at the corner of his lips, like he was trying to keep from smiling.

"You are cold. Let me help you."

I hadn't been cold, but now that he mentioned it, I was suddenly aware of the weight of my soaked clothes on my skin. Shivering, I wrapped my arms around myself, watching as the sleeve of his cloak came forward. I anticipated a hoof to appear from within the shadows and folds, but I was pleasantly surprised to find an unremarkable human hand instead.

That comforting warmth was radiating from him, tantalizing.

Reflexively, I reached out and took that hand, comforted as it wrapped around mine.

He was tall, but while enveloped in that thick midnight black cloak, he appeared small and thin. I was shocked by the strength that followed as he pulled me up and out of the water. My stomach tumbled through my abdomen, and my mouth filled with saliva. I was sure I was going to throw up, but as I rose onto my shaking legs, I tumbled into the being's arms.

Instantly, that warmth he radiated enveloped me, and the softness of his cloak seemed to do the same.

My eyelids were heavy, heavier than even my body, as I fell limply against the being's sturdy form. I was going to disappear again. I could feel it, and that fear was once again bubbling up inside me. But just as I was about to flail and panic, the being's hand began to stroke my water-soaked hair.

"Go to sleep. The next time you wake up, you'll be somewhere safer."

I had no idea who this being was, but I found myself believing him with my entire being, and with that, I let my eyes fall shut. My vision went dark, but I could still feel the intense light radiating from him. Even that disappeared as my consciousness faded away into full darkness.

CHAPTER TWO

There was warmth. My immediate, groggy thoughts were of the great being who had lifted me into his arms and held me until I fell asleep, but as I lay there, my eyes shut, I became acutely aware that this warmth wasn't as consistent or enveloping. Disturbed, I opened my eyes and found a dancing flame of red and orange, crackling as it burned through a stack of sticks within it.

I blinked, surprised.

As I sat up, my joints cracked, and a tingling sensation raced through my body as a result. Despite lying on packed dirt, I was quite comfortable and relaxed. It was a much better waking experience than what I had the last time.

Taking in my surroundings this time, I found myself in a round cave, dug deep into the stone. The fire was putting off a pleasant orange glow, but it probably wouldn't be enough to keep the darkness at bay. Thankfully, the man was sitting at the back of the cave, leaning against the cave wall, his eyes shut. Unfortunately, the antlers on his head wouldn't allow him to lie it back against the wall, so his chin was resting against his chest, the antlers jutting out from the top, their light filling the hollow space.

They were impressive, with eight tines coming off each of the main beams.

Maybe impressive wasn't the right word. They were beautiful.

Tearing my eyes away, I peered out to the other side of the cave, where it tunneled outward to the outside world. It was night outside, but the moonlight from above was beaming down, lighting the rushing water of the river outside. But that wasn't the only light. Floating along the top of the water were bright golden bulbs of light, exuding hazy white auras, bumping and bobbing along the surface.

It reminded me of the light coming from the being's antlers, and I was tempted to get up and see if I could figure out what they were. But, as if he had awoken from that very thought in my head, a grumbling voice explained:

"Those are souls."

"Souls?"

I looked back to find the being smiling, his light eyes trained on me with a knowing look.

"Yes. Souls. They are going back to the place where all living beings go when their time is up — to be with family or friends. To rest."

I could hardly believe what he was saying. Though much of me still felt lost and empty, I felt some disbelief bubbling in the pit of my stomach. I turned back to look at the river, watching as these things he called souls bobbed up and down in the water, almost like they were alive.

As I watched, one of the souls bounced a little too far out of the water, landing with a thud on the stony shore of the river. It twitched and moved for a few moments, like it was trying to work its way back to the water, only to give up and just flicker on the shore. My chest squeezed, and I was just about to get up and try to help the poor thing, only for a dark shadow to suddenly fly past me.

I blinked, watching as the being silently moved out of the cave and toward the stuck soul.

I awkwardly clambered up to my feet, trotting close behind until we reached the shore. The being stopped, stooping down to the ground, his hands slipping out from within his great sleeves. Though I had no idea what was happening or why, as the being cupped his hands beneath the glowing orb and lifted it, my stomach was turning flips in my abdomen.

I felt like I was seeing something I shouldn't.

No, like I was seeing something no human should.

Still, I found myself slack-jawed and staring, amazed by the brilliant light emanating from the ball as it settled in the being's hands.

Looking down at it, the being smiled, murmuring:

"Don't worry. I'm here to help."

And with that, he knelt forward, holding his cupped hands above the rushing water. As soon as he spread his hands, the soul fell back into the river, joining the rest of the fray. It didn't even make a sound or a splash, seamlessly joining the others. I tried my best to keep an eye on it, but the further it drifted with the rest, the harder it was to discern one orb from the other. They were all orbs, all with that same brilliant glow.

We watched in silence for a while, the being and I, but as I watched, I recalled that I had awoken in this very river of souls, with no memory of who I was or why I was there. I glanced up at the being, who I found to be staring down at me like he was awaiting the question I had yet to even ask. My face burned, and with a shaking voice, I asked:

"Do only souls appear in this river?"

He bobbed his head.

"Nothing alive or anything like that?"

He bobbed his head again.

I swallowed.

"Has any other living person appeared here?"

His response this time was delayed, his brows furrowing like he was trying to recall if he had ever seen such a thing. Eventually, he shook his head.

"Am I dead?"

This time, he didn't respond at all. He directed his attention back to the river, staring at the orbs that continued to make their way down the river to wherever they were meant to be at the end of life. My mouth was dry, and my throat constricted. I had so much more to ask, but I wasn't sure I wanted to hear the answers.

Finally, after some more time in awkward silence had passed, the being spoke again.

"I don't know why you are here. I've been alone since I appeared here. I knew I was meant to guide all the souls that appeared here to where they were meant to be in the end." His gaze shifted to me, and a comforting and knowing smile was directed my way. "You are a soul, just like any other. I'm not sure where you are meant to be, but I will guide you just like all the others."

Though he hadn't said it to me, the words he had said to the orb echoed through my mind:

"Don't worry. I'm here to help."

My face burned. I wanted to thank this being, but as I tried to work up the courage, one of his arms wrapped around my shoulder, tugging me into his warm embrace. I squeaked, shocked as his head suddenly came down to rest atop my own, nuzzling against my scalp.

I couldn't bring myself to say a word, no matter how thankful I was. So, I basked in his warmth and comfort instead, hoping to eventually find the strength within myself to say it one day.

CHAPTER THREE

As the sun rose, the light enveloped the light of the orbs in the river. Like candles being blown out, they steadily flickered out of existence, leaving the river as empty and cold as I had experienced it the day I had woken inside of it.

I asked:

"Where did they go?"

"The journey to their resting place is a long one. They have to rest — they are human, after all."

It was still hard for me to believe they were humans in any shape or form, but I didn't question it further. Instead, I wanted to find out more about the confirmed non-human next to me.

"What are you?"

His head tilted side to side as he mused over the question, and though he didn't have any, I couldn't help but imagine the flickering of deer ears on either side of his antlers. After some time, he responded:

"I don't really know. Did you not see beings like me in your world?"

I didn't have any clear recollection of where I came from, but something deep within me was sure I had never met anything or anyone quite like him. So, all I could do was shake my head.

The being hummed.

"I am a guide. That is all I knew when I was born here, and that is all I know to be now."

"What's your name then?"

As he glanced down at me, he tilted his head.

"Name?"

"What are you called?"

He shook his head.

"No one has called me anything. You are the first person I have ever spoken to who has spoken back."

My heart fluttered in my chest, and I found a skip in my step as we went around the corner of the woods, continuing along the river's edge. I liked that I might be the only one to know who this person was. It felt like I might be important to him.

Plus, though the man was so different than me, there was something we had in common that I desperately latched on to: our names. He had no name, and neither did I. There was something immensely comforting about not being the only being without an identity.

"So, you have no name. Do you know mine?"

He shook his head.

"I've never met anyone with a name."

As he spoke, that neutral and distant tone was steadily being replaced with something hollow and pained. As I peered up into his face, I found his brows furrowing and the corners of his lips twitching downward. I had so far been referring to him as a being, something inhuman, but looking at him now, he seemed painfully human.

My chest squeezed.

Swallowing, I stammered out the first thing I could think of to lighten the mood:

"We could give each other names!"

That despondent visage suddenly vanished. As his brows raised, he asked:

"Really?"

I bobbed my head so hard I felt dizzy.

"Sure, why not? We have to call each other something. I can't just be human, and you…"

As I stared into his face, which had settled back into that familiar, peaceful, and wizened expression, I found myself unable to continue. What would I call such a being? How would he react if he knew I referred to him as 'the being' to myself? The thought of that sad and lonely expression returning to his face made my stomach turn.

But what made my stomach turn all the more was his hand, as it slipped from within his cloak to grasp mine. It was bad enough if he just held it, but instead, his fingers constantly slipped between mine. His constant warmth enveloped my entire hand, but the direct touch from his flesh left trails of titillating heat everywhere they brushed. As soon as one section of my hand cooled, his fingers were back to brush right over it.

It left me wordless, openly gawking as he expectantly waited for my next words.

"Well? What would you call me?"

I wanted to say beautiful, but I thankfully caught myself.

Instead, I swallowed, carefully considering words from a past I had no recollection of. The first thing that came to mind was the sun, and what followed was the name of something that barked. Something with fur. A memory?

"Apollo?"

The being was beaming almost as bright as the light that radiated from his antlers.

21

"Apollo. I like that name."

I shook my head, realizing the name I recalled was something I once called a dog. I couldn't remember if they were my pet or just a dog I knew of, but either way, it felt wrong to call a being like this the same name I once called a pet. But as I shook my head, his face seemed to fall. There was a quiver in his bottom lip as he asked:

"Is it bad?"

With a sigh, I shook my head. Instantly, that brilliant smile returned, and he said his new name over and over again, his lips accentuating each sound with such an exaggerated expression that I had to laugh. As long as he liked it, I supposed it was as good a name as any.

But then his attention was back on me.

"But what about you? What will be your name?"

My cheeks burned. I wondered if he felt as excited and nervous when he asked me to name him as I had felt.

"I named you. It's only fair for you to name me, too."

He hummed, glancing at the river. There were no orbs that we could see, yet there seemed to be a shimmer in his eye as if he could see something I could not. It made me wonder what it felt like to be the only being in a world with all these mystical powers. I couldn't imagine the peace, but I also couldn't fathom the loneliness.

Finally, Apollo murmured.

"I don't know any names. Not for souls, anyway." He then met my gaze. "Would River be a good name?"

It was as good a name as Apollo, I supposed.

"It would, but why 'River'?"

Unsurprisingly, Apollo pointed to the river beside us. I sighed, a bit put off by how uncreative of a name it was until he explained:

"You were brought to me by the river. Every soul that comes here is a gift, but you are a special one. It was the best name I could think of."

My face burned, especially as his fingers continued to entangle with my own. Finding some courage, I grasped his hand in mine, squeezing it.

"I like it. Thank you."

Apollo beamed, chuckling as he squeezed my hand in return.

Though my hand wasn't as warm as his, and I couldn't radiate light like the souls in the river, I hoped he felt as enveloped in warmth as I did.

CHAPTER FOUR

Once again, I found myself in a small hovel, though this one was made of sticks and brush, built to form a small hutch where Apollo had built a fire. We were sitting together, watching the souls meander down the river once more. It was peaceful and pleasant.

It was also somewhat uncomfortable. I made a great effort not to touch him. Doing so made my heart race and thump so heavily against my sternum that it made me dizzy. But no matter how hard I tried to keep from carelessly touching him, my knee would occasionally brush his leg, or my shoulder would inevitably bump into him.

I jerked away as quickly as possible to create space, but that burning warmth of his lingered wherever we connected, and it was far too much for my heart to bear.

As I glanced up at him, he didn't seem to mind. In fact, he didn't seem to notice whatsoever, his attention entirely on the river instead.

That made my stomach ache all the more.

I was a mess of contradictions, which left me frustrated

on top of the sickness I was feeling.

Clearing my throat, I asked:

"Why do we stop every night? Shouldn't you be helping the souls down the river?"

Without even looking my way, he responded.

"When you appeared in the river, it was still daytime. Usually, souls sleep during the day and move at night, but you don't have a light. It made more sense for you to travel during the day instead of the night."

So, he was doing it for me.

As my knee bumped his, I suddenly wasn't so quick to pull it away.

"What about the fire? Do you need to stay warm?"

Admittedly, I knew the answer, but I still wanted to hear it all the same.

He shook his head.

"No, but you don't make heat like me or the souls. I didn't want you to be cold."

I was burning from the inside out.

I felt perfectly warm right next to him.

Blushing, I leaned over, resting my head against his arm. Reflexively, he moved. His arm went around my shoulder, nestling me into his side. His hand cradled my elbow, his thumb making small circles there. This was pleasant and comfortable. It felt like something we had done thousands of times before, and I wanted nothing more than to do it a thousand times more after this.

Just as I was settling in, nearly falling asleep, a few orbs suddenly jumped a little higher than the rest, landing on the shore. A couple rolled off the shore and back into the water, but two remained stuck along the rocks. Apollo stiffened, his legs shifting as he prepared to stand up.

Before he could, I asked:

"Can I put them back?"

Apollo stilled, glancing down at me.

"You want to help them back in?"

Still flushed, I nodded.

Apollo hummed, staring at me for a while. Then, after glancing back at the orbs, he met my gaze once more. With that gentle smile of his, he gave my arm a squeeze.

"I don't see why not."

Suddenly electric with nerves and excitement, I jumped up and trotted toward the river's edge, where the glowing orbs waited. As I neared, I glanced back, happy to find Apollo watching with a pleasant smile. Encouraged, I stooped down to pick up one of the orbs.

I did my best to mimic what he had done before, cupping the orbs from beneath and lifting them.

To my surprise, the orb was much denser than I had anticipated. Its glow was light and hazy, so I had expected my hands to go right through it, but holding it in my hands, it felt much more like a firm jelly. Even as the orb flickered, the slick jelly remained solid.

They felt more alive than they had seemed before, though they reminded me of something nonhuman — slick things that also lived in water. The word for them was escaping me, but I could recall holding them in a time before I woke up here. The memory flickered brightly in my mind, and I couldn't help smiling down at the orb in return.

Ducking my head, I whispered to the orb, hoping to emulate Apollo's comforting cadence.

"Go on now. Your family is waiting for you."

And with that, I held the orb back over the river and let it go.

It bobbed about like it was happy to rejoin its fellow souls before slipping down the river once again.

More confident now, I did the same to the second orb, scooping it up and whispering positive affirmations and encouragement before letting it join the rest of the fray. Once again, the orb bounced about among the others before being swept away.

I remained there, crouched, watching the steady flow of the water with all of the other orbs flickering in it. They were quite beautiful, and some part of me was a little jealous, having been born in this world as a human instead of something so simple yet lovely. But then I remembered Apollo.

Sure, the orbs got a lot of his attention, but they couldn't talk to him and know him like I could.

I couldn't hold back the stupid grin that fought its way to my lips, and I similarly couldn't keep myself from glancing back. There, Apollo was waiting for me. He grinned, clapping his hands like he was cheering me on.

Feeling light and fluttery, I stood up and made my way back to him, asking:

"How was that?"

As I took my seat next to him, he beamed.

"Wonderful."

Being reborn here was worth it for that little bit of recognition alone.

"Awesome. The souls are so pretty at night. They're almost like stars when they glow like that."

He hummed:

"You know, you glow, too."

"I do?"

Silent, he nodded.

My face was on fire again. I swallowed, unsure if I had the confidence to ask what I really wanted to. Finally, with nothing else to say, I stammered:

"Am I as pretty as the souls?"

He chuckled, suddenly ducking down so his lips were just barely brushing the shell of my ear.

"Don't tell the others, but you are the prettiest soul I've seen."

Though he did straighten up, putting a bit of distance between us, my entire body was positively burning. Still, though I was happy to hear he thought I was pretty, the word soul left a bitter taste in my mouth.

Was I just another soul born in this world for him to guide?

As I stared up at him, watching as he stared at the souls, I wasn't so sure the look he was giving them was so different than the one he gave me. My chest was tight, even as I eventually settled down to sleep the rest of the night.

CHAPTER FIVE

By the time I woke up, the sun was hanging low in the sky. My schedule was gradually aligning with Apollo's, though it seemed he didn't sleep as often as I did, if at all. The only time I had seen an inkling of him being tired was in the cave. Since then, I had scarcely seen him with his eyes closed.

As soon as I woke up, he was usually awake, waiting for me.

Today was no different.

As I opened my eyes, I found his already open and trained on me. He greeted me with a smile, one that stirred my heart.

"Did you sleep well?"

I swallowed, trying to keep my voice steady as I nodded:

"I did. Did you?"

He positively beamed, nodding in return. Wordlessly, he stood up and steadily began to make his way toward me. Enveloped in his cloak, he seemed to float, leaving me breathless until he was hovering above me. The light from his antlers, like a halo, seemed to beam down from above, illuminating the planes of his face.

I couldn't help it. The first thing that came to mind was that he was beautiful.

My face was burning, and it took far too much effort to choke back the urge to touch him, especially as he proffered his hand to help me up.

"Can I help you up?"

I wanted nothing more than to grab that hand and squeeze it. I wanted to feel his warmth soak into me and fill me. Then, I wanted to fill him with my own warmth and hope he felt the same.

These embarrassing thoughts were fleeting, leaving me horrified by my flights of fancy.

Choking back my pitiful stutters, I waved away his hand and awkwardly clambered up onto my feet instead. But no matter how much I tried to avoid his touch, as soon as I was up, those warm hands were cupping my elbows, pulling me so close that the aura of warmth around him instantly enveloped me. I couldn't bring myself to meet his eyes, worried I might embarrass myself further.

Where the edges of his cloak were loosely tied together, the view of his bare chest had my heart leaping up into my throat. The skin was smooth and completely unmarred. Plus, it had a visible suppleness to it that suggested if I were to press my fingers into it, they would sink right in.

My head was spinning, and the pleasant silence was maddening.

With weak tugs, I put some distance between us — just enough so I could gather my thoughts and try to fill the air between us with something other than my deafening heartbeat.

"So, um." I coughed. "Shall we go?"

He didn't respond right away, his hands still cupping

my elbows, kneading them there for a while before finally bobbing his head.

"Yes. Let's go."

And with that, he let me go, moving aside so he could head toward the river's edge, where we would start our walk once more. His intense heat dissipated almost instantly, leaving me uncomfortably cold. I couldn't help wrapping my arms around myself, cupping my arms, missing the warmth that I had made a point to get away from.

I found myself frustrated.

I was frustrated by how much I longed to be closer to him, yet how intensely I wanted to put distance between us simply because I was too afraid to be close to him. He was an otherworldly being, and I was a simple human. I didn't know who I was, much less who he was.

Everything about this strange relationship we had felt dangerous for innumerable reasons, but it felt so right all the same.

It felt like I was meant to be here with him.

But did I have any right to feel that way?

All of these contradictory feelings, wants, and needs had my stomach turning. Frowning, I tried my best to leave them all behind as I took my place at Apollo's side by the river's edge.

As usual, we walked for a while in complete silence, the sounds of the river and wind rustling through the trees as our backdrop. This was beginning to feel routine, like we had done it a thousand times before and would do it a thousand times after this, but in that way, it felt purposeless. Beyond helping the souls at night, I couldn't discern why we were walking these lengths each day and night.

As I peered up at Apollo, I found his gaze already focused on me. Knowing he had been watching me while my mind wandered made my face burn. With a cough, I asked:

"So, where are we going?"

To my surprise, his pleasant visage faltered. It was only for a moment, but that soft smile he seemed to have permanently fixed on his face twitched downward. His eyebrows followed suit. It was a look of pain or disgust — I couldn't be certain which, as his reaction was quickly replaced with the constant state of peace he had, though now it seemed much more put on and hollow.

As he looked forward, breaking our eye contact, I found that I was able to breathe more easily, as if a scary stranger had finally left.

Finally, he responded:

"To the end."

He had mentioned this before. Still, I asked:

"Where the souls go to rest?"

He nodded, his attention trained entirely forward, though it seemed from the emptiness in his eyes that he wasn't really seeing what was ahead of us. It was like he wasn't beside me at all. He was somewhere much farther away, and I felt terrifyingly alone.

Was this how he had felt before I appeared here?

Part of me hoped not, but another part of me hoped that meant I was a comfort to him in some way — that I was an important fixture in his existence.

He nodded.

"Yes."

"Why?"

He shrugged, though he still answered:

"It's my best guess as to where you need to go."

I stumbled, which prompted his hand to suddenly reach out, grasping my side and pulling me to him to keep me up. Still, I ended up stumbling over my words:

"W-where I need to go?"

"Yes."

I tried to stop, but I was still tethered to Apollo's side, and though he appeared soft and gentle, he continued to pull me along beside him. If he was taking me to the end, it didn't seem like there was anything I could do to stop him.

"Why would I need to go anywhere?"

He was refusing to look at me, though his face continued to contort. He was openly frowning, his eyes narrowing like he was staring into the sun, though it was steadily disappearing behind the horizon.

"All souls have to leave this place. It's how it's meant to be."

And as if on cue, the river began to twinkle with souls flickering into existence. As I watched them, I couldn't help but note how different they were from me. Yet, Apollo called me a soul, just like them. But unlike them, as they happily bobbed down the river to the end of their journey, I wasn't so sure that was where I ultimately belonged.

"What if I don't want to go?"

Finally, he stopped, directing his full attention to me. His eyes, sparkling gold, seemed to wander around in their socket, lost and unsure where to look. His lips pursed just before he murmured:

"I don't know."

I didn't know either. What was I brought here for? What was the point?

Maybe it was all just a fluke, and I was destined to go where all souls went. There was no one like me here. Maybe I didn't belong.

Yet, as I stared into Apollo's face, his expression lost, I felt that need again. I reached up, cupping his face between my palms, welcomed once more by his never-ending warmth. His countenance relaxed, eyes fluttering shut as he nestled into my hands.

"Won't you be lonely?"

His eyes opened once more, but instead of that warm glow that radiated from within him, his gaze was steely and distant.

"Yes, but I've always been alone."

And just like that, I was chilled. Apollo pulled away, leaving me standing alone. He stepped forward, taking much longer strides than he had been, leaving me alone along the river's edge. As I stood there in the cold night air, illuminated by the light of the souls traveling down the river, I was once more pressed by how lonely and painful it all was.

If the guide of this world felt I was meant to go to the end, who was I to say otherwise?

And yet, as I watched his silhouette gliding down the river's edge, I felt compelled to follow him — not to the end, but for as long as he walked along the shore. Surely, this feeling wasn't just my own selfish need to be with Apollo for however long I was able.

But I had no way to confirm these feelings. All I could do was jog to Apollo and take my place back by his side. We continued to walk in silence to an end I wasn't sure was mine.

CHAPTER SIX

The silence wasn't unpleasant when paired with his heat, but it was much more hollow than it had been in the short time we had been traveling together. Before, as we walked, we would often brush against each other's shoulders, arms, and sides. I would usually jump away, nervous. However, this time, any time our bodies so much as had a whisper of contact, he was wincing away from *me*, like I was the one emitting enough heat to burn him.

My heart, not unlike the souls in the river beside us, bobbed about in my chest.

I hated that I had tried so hard to avoid his touch. If I had known that he would eventually put a wall between us, I would've relished every chance I got to be close to him. Wherever the end was, it was clear he was trying to put distance between us for when we eventually got there. I could only presume this would mean the end of our travels together, forever.

It was a thought that made my mouth run dry.

Once again, his hand brushed mine, and he jolted away,

taking a full step to the side to put more distance between us. Inevitably, like magnets, as we walked side-by-side, we would gradually get closer and closer once again. But this time, as his hand brushed mine, and I felt the twitch of his finger, ready to pull away, I grabbed his hand, squeezing it into my own.

I expected him to jump and yank away, maybe more violently than he had when we just brushed. But to my surprise, his hand squeezed mine in return. I stared up into his face, determined to find some meaning there, only to find him still staring straight ahead, toward an end I couldn't see. But within his glowing eyes, I could make out the glistening of tears.

I wanted to ask what they were for, but the words were stuck in my throat.

It burned so painfully through my chest and in my face that my eyes were brimming with their own tears. I coughed, squeezing Apollo's hand all the same, knowing well now that this would probably be the very last time.

By the time we made it to the bend at the river, our hands were sopping wet from sweat. My other hand wasn't fairing much better, wet with tears instead, as I hopelessly tried to wipe them away. Apollo was much stronger than I was. Though his eyes had been sparkling with unshed tears for a while, not one escaped that I could see.

I wanted to ask him why he felt he had to take me to the end. I wanted to ask him if he would miss me, and then I wanted to tell him he didn't have to. We didn't have to go there. He didn't have to let me go. Unlike the souls we traveled with, I didn't feel compelled to go there, so maybe I wasn't meant to.

But as we walked along the bend, there before us was the end. I had been so used to the thick, plush grass, the stony, gravelly river shore, and the never-ending line of trees that seeing anything else was a shock. There was a long stretch of white sand, invoking shadowy memories of laughter, dogs barking, and cold drinks that were cold going down but warmed me from the inside out.

This was a beach.

Except there, in the center of what should have been an ocean where the river let out, was a large cyclone of water, pulling all of the souls from the river down into a seemingly never-ending spiral. The light of the orbs wobbled and flickered all the way down before disappearing entirely out of sight. Apollo, undisturbed, stepped closer, and as I followed, I found something within me flickering.

Heat in the pit of my stomach was bubbling outward, as if it were stomach acid trying to burn through my flesh.

I glanced down, startled by the pain, only to be more shocked by a light radiating from my abdomen.

Panicked, I pressed against the light like I was trying to hold myself together, but nothing would stop the light as it grew and grew, brighter and brighter, bleeding through my fingers.

I looked to Apollo, hoping for some help, only to find him staring at me. His brows were turned downward, his lips following suit. He looked like someone who was in mourning, and I couldn't fathom why.

"I have to guide souls to their resting place. You are a soul, too."

Shaking my head, I tried to take a step back, only for my foot to suddenly step forward. As the light tugged forward, my body followed. I stepped closer and closer to the ocean's shore, passing Apollo as I went. His gaze was locked on me, watching with immense sadness as I went.

Though, for a brief instance, as I neared him, his hand reached out, brushing my arm. At that moment, I felt the warmth within me shift, trying to re-enter me. It wanted to reach his warmth and join it. But as soon as his touch was gone, so too was the will of my light — my soul. It went back to pulling me towards the end, where cold water splashed up, peppering my face in icy droplets that burned more than any heat ever could.

The water was dark and churning, but the souls seemed to willingly fall deeper and deeper inside. All of their former jostling and hopping had ceased, replaced by stillness as they appeared to accept the fate before them. They had traveled all this way, and it was finally time for them to rest.

Maybe I was supposed to join them.

Watching as their light disappeared into the darkness, where all of their family and friends waited, where they could wait for the inevitable rebirth and start of a new journey. It sounded so pleasant that it was hard for me not to want to give in and join them.

But then I peered back.

I looked over my shoulder, expecting Apollo to be waiting for me to go on with a smile, much like he had done with every other soul he had helped back on their journey to the end. Instead, there I saw this once-bright being, now less so. His light was radiant as ever, but his eyes were dim. His lips were hardened into a neutral line, and he felt like he was miles and miles away from me.

PART TWO

THE BEING

CHAPTER SEVEN

My breath hitched in my throat as our eyes met.

His eyes were a deep umber. They were so dark, they were almost pitch, and they had an endless quality to them that drew my attention any time he was looking my way. There was nothing like the night sky, especially during the day. Yet, there he was before me, a human being with what appeared to be the night in his eyes.

But as his soul was being pulled away, called to where I thought it was meant to go, the sparkling midnight in his gaze flickered away to a cold ash.

Never in all my time as I helped soul after soul make their way to the end, where they were meant to be, had I ever once questioned what I was doing. From the moment I gained consciousness, I knew what my purpose was. There was no reason to doubt it.

But there had never been something— *someone* like River before.

I had been foolishly referring to him as another soul and assumed that where he needed to be was where all of the other souls needed to go.

But as his form faded, his lips forming my name before being replaced by that familiar orb of light that all souls were made of, I reached out to him. I wanted nothing more than to snatch him back toward the forest where he would be safe from the pull of the end. But it was too late.

In a blink, the orb that was River joined the others in the cyclone, bobbing up and down among them until I couldn't discern it from any of the others. And just like that, he was gone. It was like he had never existed, to begin with.

This should have been fine. This was how it had always been. The world was as it should be once more. I was alone; the souls were on their journey to where they belonged, and I could go back to helping all those who were beginning that same journey.

But as I turned to leave and head back into the denser forest along the river's edge, I peered back over my shoulder. Some part of me expected him to still be standing there, his cheeks burning red while his lips twitched up into a small, tight smile. I wanted to be able to reach out and hold him, to feel the gradual shift from his chilly flesh to my never-ending warmth.

I wanted to hear his voice and watch him react to things.

But he was no longer there.

It was an empty beach, just as it always had been.

Just as it always would be.

There was something in my chest, lurching up into my throat. I wanted to choke and gag, but there was no reason to do so. I swallowed instead, only to find a dense and heavy lump falling into the pit of my stomach.

Dizzy, I faced forward once more. Each step was wobbly and unsteady, more unsure than they had ever been. The heaviness in my abdomen was throwing me off balance, and there was nothing I could do to stop it. Not now.

By the time I made it back onto the grassy earth, the sun was beginning to rise. The light from the river was steadily being replaced by the light of the sun, but the darkness that burned within me was much greater than either of them. Part of me was thankful that the sun had risen, as the night sky was a painful reminder of the eyes that had blinked out of existence right before me. No wonder humans came to this place as souls. Knowing the name and face of the soul was just too painful to say goodbye to.

All I needed to do was rest, like I used to.

When the sun rose, I would rest, whether conscious or not, and wait until the sun had set. Then, I could get back to what I was meant to do. Time would pass like it always did, and the souls would call to me like they always did: silently.

Never again would I hear the name 'Apollo.'

Never again would I have to call out 'River.'

My world would be silent once more, and I could focus on what mattered: guiding.

My hoof slipped, and I was too sick to catch myself. In a great rush of wind, as the thickness of my cloak crumpled beneath me, I hit the earth. Everything inside me quaked, leaving me more shaken than I had been on my uneven hooves. I gasped, unable to catch my breath.

Through a cacophony of stimulation, including bleary eyes and an incessant ringing in my ears, I caught sight of one of my tines lying in the grass. The light radiating from it flickered once. Twice. Then, it faded to nothing. It was just another thing I had lost.

Glancing around, I was surrounded by the trees I had known for my entire being. They had been my friends and silent confidants, but now the silence was deafening, and their forms were strangers. My eyes were rolling aimlessly in their sockets, sending everything spinning until it all went black.

Black like the night sky.
Black like River's eyes.
It was all gone.
I had lost my light.

PART THREE

THE SOUL

CHAPTER EIGHT

I had been here before.

I didn't recognize it by what I could see. Though maybe 'seeing' wasn't quite the right word. It was more like I was experiencing things. There were flickers of things — some more concrete than others.

It would be colors. Sometimes a gradient. Sometimes solid and opaque. Others like a smudge of a million different shades.

Then there were feelings. It would be a rush of immense joy to the point I could feel the pain of stitches in my sides, though I had no form to experience such things.

I could hear a dog barking, and the name Apollo would come to mind, only to be replaced by a ghost of someone I once knew, who was also called by that same name. I could feel the burning of embarrassment, realizing this person shared the same name as a dog.

Then there were voices.

They called out to me, beckoning me closer, and though I was compelled to go to them, there was a part of me that wanted to linger in the unknown.

So, *they* came to me.

It was a face. A solid face with a strong jawline and a heavy brow. His nose bore a resemblance to mine, and his eyes were a dark shade. It felt a bit like looking into the surface of the river. It looked like me, but unlike me at the same time.

He smiled.

"I didn't know when I'd see you again, but I didn't want it to be so soon."

I didn't have a heart, but I was sure it would be heavy if I did.

And if I had a head, I would've shaken it, unsure of who this was or what his words meant, but he was undeterred by my silence.

"You've come before your mother. I didn't want to leave her alone with you, but now she's even more alone without you."

His face wilted, and to my surprise, I found that I had hands and they suddenly grasped the face. The face smiled again, though much weaker than before. His brows were furrowed, and his lips trembled, but he smiled all the same.

"You're not quite one of us yet, are you?"

I wasn't even sure *who* he was, much less *what* he was. Still, I felt sure that he was right. Whatever he was, I wasn't quite there yet.

Recognizing that, I found that I had a voice, too.

"Who are you?"

His face fell again, and this time, I had a heart whose weight was almost too much to carry. I must have had a face for him to see my feelings, as the words that followed were painfully comforting.

"Don't worry. I'm someone you knew and who knew you a long time ago."

Suddenly, amid the darkness, another face appeared. This one was much older. She had creases around her eyes, which were bright and alert, like sapphires. When she smiled, a flurry of wrinkles appeared across her face, but she had a youthful and sly upturn at the corner of her mouth.

"My, my. Long time, no see."

Again, a face that felt familiar, but wholly unfamiliar at the same time.

Suddenly, she whistled.

"Daniel, he's grown up to look just like you. It's a shame he's come here so young."

Again, the man's face crumpled.

I was compelled to ask this new face:

"Who are you?"

That bright and brilliant expression suddenly twisted in something akin to disgust. She shook her head, frowning.

"You have to be kidding. I changed your diapers, kid."

Though I had asked, it was clear to me even before that I was close to these people, whoever they were. But no matter how hard I tried, I couldn't manifest any memory of these people.

I did have experiences, though. There was laughter. I was partially submerged in cold, clear water. There was a voice, like hers, calling to me, but I couldn't hear what. Then, the dog barked again. There was splashing.

The man, Daniel, frowned at the woman, shaking his head in disapproval.

"Mother. If he doesn't remember, he doesn't remember. Stranger things have happened here."

The woman stuck her tongue out, but there was a sadness in her eyes. They sparkled and shimmered, like they were full of unshed tears.

Daniel then directed his attention back to me.

"So, you're not like us, and yet you're here. What's

brought you here?"

What had brought me here? There was something in the back of my mind. It was fuzzy and distant, but it was there. I closed my eyes, thrusting myself into complete darkness where the image steadily came into focus.

There was sand. My feet were sinking into it, and splashing on the shore were the waves from a vortex, spinning and spinning down into an inky blackness. However, speckled across the darkness were golden orbs, flickering and bouncing around amid the raging water. As I stared, I could feel something in the pit of my stomach pulling.

It was beckoning me forward.

I wanted to go to it. I felt like something or someone was waiting for me. But as I clutched my stomach, trying to hold myself together, I peered back over my shoulder.

There, standing behind me, was someone else. It was another person who felt familiar, but whose name I couldn't place.

My eyes were burning, tears threatening to spill.

He looked so terribly sad.

It was then that something clicked. I remembered barking — a dog. There was a man who, unfortunately, was named after a dog.

Apollo.

I opened my eyes, gasping. My chest was heaving. Daniel and the woman were staring at me, their brows furrowed. It was in this moment that I realized how similar they looked to each other.

My voice wavered as I said:

"I was guided here."

Daniel nodded.

"We all were. By the guide."

Yes, it was the guide. *He* was the guide to this world,

and if I were a soul like any other, he was supposed to bring me here.

But if that was true, why did he look so sad?

And why did I still feel compelled to look back?

The woman squinted, and some part of me felt like all of my greatest secrets were on display. I shivered as she asked:

"Did you meet the guide?"

Again, I remembered things randomly.

His warmth. His arms. His light.

His smile.

But also, that deep sadness.

Yes, I had met the guide, but I didn't *know* the guide.

But I wanted to.

Daniel's face lit up, while mine burned.

"Oh. It looks like you did. We've felt his warmth and heard him speak, but we've never seen him."

The woman's eyes widened along with her grin.

"Oh? Was he handsome? Was he as kind to you as he was to us?"

I recalled him lifting me out of the water, like I weighed nothing. There was unending warmth he shared with me in small, gentle touches. There was the warmth our bodies shared as we sat together in his small hovel, as if the entire world was comprised of just the two of us.

Well, it had just been the two of us. No one else existed in that world but us.

Yet, now I was here, and that meant Apollo was all alone once more.

Finally, I looked back.

There was unending darkness. It was all-consuming, and the weight of it was crushing. Instantly, all the want I had to return to where I had been, and to where Apollo was waiting for me, evaporated. I was compelled to look forward and continue to where I was meant to go.

But just as I turned to face those who were still watching me, I saw a flicker.

It was a small, fuzzy light, but it was there.

It was calling to me. I was sure of it, and when I faced Daniel and the woman's faces, still floating in the darkness, I said as such:

"I need to go back."

The woman gasped, shaking her head in disbelief.

"Go back? How the hell do you expect to—"

Daniel hissed.

"Mother." The woman stopped, and with a sigh, Daniel directed his attention back to me. "Why would you need to go back?"

My face was burning, my heart thrumming so hard I thought I might just fly up into the darkness whether I wanted to or not.

I swallowed.

"There's someone... the guide. He needs me. He's all alone, and I think..."

I wasn't sure what else to say, as my heart squeezed in my chest.

Looking at these two faces, whose names I didn't know beyond what I had heard them say to each other, yet who seemed to know me intimately well, I felt like I *should* want to be with them. I felt like there was a time when I would've abandoned anyone or anything to be with them.

But they were strangers to me now. Yet, that didn't make it hurt any less.

"I'm sorry. I need to go back."

Daniel was smiling, though there was sadness in the angle of his brow. Still, he shook his head.

"There's no need to apologize. We'll help you however we can."

The woman sighed, rolling her eyes.

"Well, whatever. If you're both so determined."

And with that, she puckered her lips and blew, releasing a high-pitched whistle. Suddenly, amid the darkness, several golden lights began to flicker into existence. Within those lights, more faces appeared. This time, I recognized none of them, but a few seemed to recognize Daniel and the woman. Watching them smile and greet each other, laughing and enjoying each other's company, I knew for sure that what I was doing was right.

They didn't need me here.

Apollo did.

I was prepared to leave, however they planned to do it, but then I met Daniel's gaze. His eyes were glistening with tears. He sniffled, holding them back. In a scratchy voice, he said:

"Before you go, we know who you are. Would you like to know, too?"

I was tempted, but I shook my head.

"No."

"Why?"

I swallowed, pressing my hands to my chest.

"I like who I am now." I smiled, recalling Apollo's face as he called me River for the first time. "I lost myself once and don't want to lose myself again."

My face burned as the following words tumbled out of my mouth:

"And the one who is waiting for me knows *this* me."

A tear fell from Daniel's eye, though wicked away by something I couldn't see.

"He's quite lucky."

The image of Apollo, bumping his forehead against mine, smiling, bloomed in the forefront of my thoughts.

"I'm lucky, too."

Daniel nodded and said nothing more to me, instead

directing his attention to the crowd of faces behind him and the woman.

"My son needs help. Will you help him?"

There was a rush of silent nods along with some murmurs of incredulity, but all agreed.

The word 'son' conjured some things. It was more of those vague images and feelings — someone warm, the smell of something sweet and sugary. Laughter, but also tears. It warmed me deep inside, from the inside out, and my vision was swimming.

I sniffed, drawing Daniel's attention again.

He tutted, shaking his head.

"Don't cry. This is a good thing."

Sure, it was a good thing for *me*, but I could feel that it might not be a good thing for *him*. To this version of me, he was a stranger, but there was a version of me he had known that he cared for dearly, and who clearly cared for him. It was painful, whether it was good for me or not.

Holding back tears, I muttered:

"I'm sorry again for leaving. I feel like you've been waiting for me."

Daniel smiled, shaking his head.

"Here, we're never lonely, so waiting isn't so bad. Take your time. Enjoy what life has to offer out there, and when you're ready, we'll be here."

And, manifesting out of nowhere, came a pair of hands beneath Daniel's face. They held my face, pulling me forward so our foreheads could touch. His eyes stared into mine, which might have made me nervous before, but instead filled me with immense comfort.

He chuckled.

"I just want you to be happy, son. That's all you need to do."

My eyes slid shut. All of the warmth and burning

happiness radiating inside me was lulling me into unconsciousness. I was happy. I was incredibly happy, and I knew I could be even happier if I could share this happiness with Apollo.

PART FOUR

THE BEING

CHAPTER NINE

They were calling me.

The souls were calling.

But it wasn't like it usually was. It was more. There were many souls, not two or three, not four or five. There were more. There were many.

There were thousands, and all of them were calling for me.

My eyes shot open and immediately landed on the piece of antler glowing on the ground. No, it wasn't glowing. It was positively radiating, exploding with light.

With a shaking hand, I plucked it from the grass, shocked by how warm it was.

The tines still attached to my head were reacting so intensely that they were shaking, coursing down the main beam, and, in turn, shaking my skull. I stood up and steadied myself as best I could, expecting to be bombarded from all sides as all of the souls from all across the river's shores called to me, but that was not the case. Instead, they were all calling from one direction.

I turned, facing the place I had so desperately tried to escape from: the end.

They were calling me from the end.

Never, in all my time of guiding, had I been called there. I naturally wound up there from time to time as I traveled up and down the river's edge, but by the time the souls made it there, I was no longer needed. The end was in sight; they knew where to go.

Yet, they were calling to me.

Stumbling, I made my way down the river's edge until I was met with the sight of the cyclone again. But more impressive than the never-ending force was what was sitting there along the ocean shore. Stuck in the sand were piles and piles of souls, flickering and blinking like twinkling stars, and more were steadily rising out of the cyclone and joining them.

It made no sense. The cyclone pulled things in; it didn't push things out.

I pushed through the sand and made my way closer to the shore, unsure whether I should try to put the souls back in first or check the vortex in the water when the decision was made for me. Suddenly, from the edge of the whirlpool, a single soul bubbled up over the edge.

It bobbed up and down as if it were about to be swept back down, only for it to suddenly jump back up. Beneath it were any number of souls rising against the current, pushing this single soul up and over the edge. All the while, the tine in my hand shook and burned.

Even though I knew I wouldn't get an answer, I cried out:

"What are you doing?"

As expected, all that followed was the splashing and coursing of water.

But, as if in response, the soul being carried up and over

the whirlpool was suddenly tossed over the water, flying through the air, unlike any other soul I had ever seen. Reflexively, I raced toward the beach, hands outstretched. Just as that ball of light was falling into my hands, a vision flickered into view, obscuring it completely.

What crashed into my hands and arms was not the little dense ball of life that was a soul, but something chilly and truly alive instead.

His body fell into mine, sending us both tumbling back into the sand. His limbs were flailing about, much like they had when I first saw him appear in the middle of the river. Back then, I treated him just like any other soul — I watched, letting him do what he may, waiting to help when he needed, but no further.

Now was different, though.

I wasn't going to just stand by and let things happen. Not again. Not when I could grab and hold him like I could right now.

My arms encircled him, squeezing his body so tightly to mine that there was a moment I thought we might meld together, and some part of me would've preferred that. If he and I were one soul, I never had to watch him disappear again.

The weight of him crashing into me was painful, elbows and limbs stabbing into me and sending me reeling backward. My feet sank into the sand, throwing my balance off. Though the sand was soft as my feet sank into it, it was like my back was hitting stone when I fell. The wind in my lungs was forced out, rushing out in a strained wheeze.

My vision was swimming with tears, both from pain and from relief, as my hands pressed into River's back. The pain in my back, shoulder, and hips was like a large, throbbing bruise, but the relief in my soaring heart was worth every ounce of it.

River stirred, craning his neck up so I could see his face. As soon as I saw his eyes, those deep brown eyes, alive and well once more, the unshed tears spilled forward. Meanwhile, River's face screwed up in shock, the apples of his cheek and the bridge of his nose blooming red.

"Am I heavy? Are you hurt? Let me—"

He began to move off of me, gingerly pressing into my chest with his palms to push himself off. The minute amount of space he put between us let the cold rush in, recalling that feeling I had when I was alone without him. Goosebumps raced across my flesh, and my stomach churned. I was getting sick again, and the only relief was River.

So, I pressed my hands into his upper back, pressing him back down into me.

"No. It's fine. Stay. Please."

He was stiff for a while, his heart thrumming so hard I could feel it pounding against my body. But as silence fell around us, except for the rushing of the water from the end and the river, his form steadily melted. Eventually, we were just lying together, unmoving except for the gradual rise and fall of our chests. My body ached, and the souls were still crying for me, making my head hurt.

But with River in my arms, I was perfectly content.

Unfortunately, we couldn't remain that way forever. I could feel time slipping away, the morning getting closer and closer as the souls on the shore waited for their turn to go to the end. As much as I didn't want to, I gave River a shake.

"I'm sorry. We need to get up and help the souls before morning."

Much to my disappointment, River jumped up, his face still burning red.

"Oh, you're right. Let's hurry and—" but as he shifted off of me onto the beach, his eyes fell to the sand and widened. I followed his gaze to find my broken tine lying there. While I was sure it was surprising to him, I couldn't anticipate the emotional reaction that followed. River's bottom lip quivered just before he sucked it into his mouth. In a quivering voice, he exclaimed:

"Oh my gosh. Did I do that? I'm so sorry, Apollo, I didn't mean—"

It was then that I realized he thought he had caused it. Sitting up, I grabbed his upper arms, drawing his shimmering eyes back to me.

"No, no, River. It wasn't you."

But nothing would stop the large tears that poured down his face. Flustered, I wasn't sure what to do. Glancing over at the tine still lying in the sand, the culprit of all this, I snatched it up and pushed it into his hands. His quivering fingers wrapped around it, its light emanating from between his fingers.

He sniffled, staring down at it.

"It's warm."

I nodded, wrapping my hands around his. They were usually chilly, but they were warming from the tine in his hands.

"It's part of me."

His eyes drifted up, gaze meeting mine.

"Can I keep it?"

Of course, he could. I'd give him everything if I could. But there was a part of me that was frustrated with his obsession over this little part of me.

"You can have all of me if you want."

His eyes went wide. Then, suddenly, with one hand, he grasped the back of my head and pulled me forward. Our lips crashed together so hard that they ached. His mouth moved against mine, opening and closing. Reflexively, I found myself doing the same, but for what purpose, I wasn't sure.

But as his tongue slipped into my mouth and coaxed my tongue out, I realized exactly why we were doing this. It was a simple one: it felt amazing.

More amazing than that was a foreign warmth invading me. I was so used to my warmth leeching into everything around me that to feel an unfamiliar one made me jump. I hadn't intended to, and I was intensely disappointed when River pulled away in response, letting his warmth fade from within me.

His eyes were narrowed, their depths swimming.

His thumbs were caressing the apples of my cheeks, a pleasant feeling, but it wasn't what I wanted. I couldn't tear my eyes away from his lips, which sparkled with a wet sheen.

"I'm sorry. Did that scare you?"

I shook my head, unsure of what to do with my hands. So I mimicked him, grasping his face between my palms. Our arms were tangling, forming a cage around us as we held each other. It felt like we were alone in our own little world. Well, in some ways, we truly were in our own little world.

"No. Do it again."

His lips turned up, then opened. My eyes fell shut once more, welcoming that soft feeling of his mouth pressing against mine. We remained locked like that for a while yet, his tongue and my tongue shifting back and forth between our mouths. All the while, that unfamiliar warmth burned within me.

I had enjoyed my warmth seeping into River. But having his warmth overtake my own was much more satisfying. I no longer felt like a sole guide, but a pair with someone else.

I was not one being.

We were one, and I would never be alone again.

After kissing for much longer than we should have, we finally made our way to the pile of souls still desperately calling us. River still had my broken tine clutched in his hand, smiling every time it shook and flickered because of the souls. We should have been picking them up and returning them to the water, but admittedly, I was overwhelmed by the sheer number of them.

I was also still bewildered by how such a thing could have occurred.

Once again, I found myself watching River.

Something in my stomach was doing flips, and I wanted nothing more than to grab him and press our mouths together again. It took far more effort than it should have to stay focused on what mattered.

Clearing my throat, I tried to focus.

"How did you do this?"

River didn't look up, crouching down to lift up a single soul of many.

"What?"

That frustration was back. I didn't like how obsessed he was over the tine. I didn't like how he admired and doted on the souls. All of my attention was on him, and I longed for his attention to be on me. Never in all of my existence had I felt compelled to be so selfish.

"How did you get back here? From the end."

He beamed, his thumbs brushing the sides of the flickering orb in his hands.

"The souls."

"The souls?"

Finally, he looked up, his night-colored eyes making my heart leap up into my throat.

"The souls guided me back to you."

The souls had guided him. It was ironic, really. They

were meant to be guided by me, and yet they had somehow guided what I lost back to me.

I took my place beside him, crouching down to be closer to him and the souls.

"Were you aware when you were a soul?"

It felt silly. I had lived alongside these things from the moment I became aware, yet I knew so little about them. For once, I was curious about them beyond guiding them.

River hummed, carefully setting the orb closer to the water. As if the ocean were aware, its waves gradually overtook more and more of the shoreline until the soul was lifted by the water and carried back out into the vortex. We were silent, watching as it disappeared out of sight, and only then did River respond.

"I'm not sure if I would call it being 'aware.'" He lifted another soul, staring into its never-ending light. "I was ready to leave. I could feel I had somewhere I was supposed to go, and there were... images."

"Images?"

He bobbed his head.

"I could see people waiting for me. I didn't recognize them, but part of me wanted to be with them. They were there, in the end." He swiped at his eyes. There were no tears, but his eyes were shimmering. "But there were images of you."

My heart leaped.

"Me?"

His face was flushed.

"Yes. I could see you alone here, and I felt like you needed me here more."

"So you came back?"

He shook his head.

"No. I couldn't. Not alone, anyway." Then, he held up the soul nestled between his hands, smiling as he showed it to me. "I saw them, too. They came to me, and together, we made our way back."

It made little sense. The vortex was powerful for a reason. Once a soul made it to the end, they were destined for rest. They need no longer suffer on the journey. A single soul shouldn't have the strength to—

But then I realized. A single soul might not have the strength alone, but many very well might. And if anyone could bring together souls, my River certainly would be the one. I placed my hands beneath River's, lifting them and the soul between us.

"We should thank them before we send them on their way."

River was sparkling.

"Yes. We should."

And so, he knelt down, whispering his thanks for their help before we set them closer to the shore's edge, watching as they were swept back into the vortex, to where they were meant to be. We did this over and over again, steadily clearing the shore of souls and sharing our thanks before sending them on their way. By the time we were done, the horizon was growing red with the light of dawn.

We stood together, side-by-side, as River yawned.

"Sorry. I didn't realize how long that would take."

I couldn't help myself, staring intently at his lips as he spoke. I couldn't be sure, but they seemed plumper. Were they bruised?

My fingers were pressed against them before I even knew what I was doing. River blinked, staring up at me wide-eyed. I immediately yanked my hand away, flailing and unsure of what to say to explain what I was doing or why. But then River grabbed my hand.

He pulled it to his face, a light blush blooming across his cheeks and the bridge of his nose. Gingerly, he pressed my palm to his mouth, where I could feel the light puckering of his lips, followed by a noisy squealing sound. It made something in my stomach flip, and I was compelled to pull my hand away and press my lips to his instead.

But River pulled my hand away and lowered his face, hiding it from my view.

Worried, I held his chin, lifting it with little resistance, only to find what had been a soft flush of red across his cheeks and nose had spread in a rush of red across his entire face. His dark eyes were wide, shifting back and forth between meeting my gaze and looking anywhere else entirely. He had always been cute, but this might have been the cutest I had ever seen him.

Unable to hold myself back any longer, I ducked down and pressed my lips to his.

He was stiff against me for a while as I held my lips to his, but eventually, he seemed to melt against me. His arms wrapped around my shoulders, pulling me to him, and to my surprise, his tongue, hot and wet, stroked against the seam between my lips.

Reflexively, I pulled away.

Sure, we had done this once already, but more clear-headed than I had been before, I wasn't sure *what* or *why* we were doing it. Curious, I asked:

"What is this?"

River blinked, his mouth partially open as he panted.

"We're kissing."

"Kissing?"

"Yeah, open your mouth."

I did as I was told, and immediately, River pressed his mouth to mine, though this time, his tongue invaded. It burned as it brushed along the inside of my mouth, sliding along my own tongue, as if it was coaxing it up to do the same. I was compelled. I slipped my tongue into his mouth.

Again, I was shocked by the sudden wave of warmth that filled me.

It felt like we were truly one being. I was taking in parts of River, just as he was taking in parts of me. I never wanted this feeling to stop, and thankfully, River didn't seem to want to either. Steadily, we tumbled down into the sand, breaking our kiss just long enough to breathe and get settled before we found each other again.

We kissed and kissed.

We kissed until the sun had long risen, and even then, we didn't stop.

PART FIVE

RIVER

CHAPTER TEN

We walked down the river's edge, hand-in-hand, scanning the water for any soul that might have mistakenly washed ashore along the rocks. The tine hanging around my neck would react whenever a soul needed guiding, just like the remaining ones atop Apollo's head. Yet, no matter how many times I told him I could go and do it myself, he was right there beside me, helping the souls back on their journey.

I often wondered why I was chosen to be by Apollo's side in this world. I had a few echoes of memories from my life as a human, but none that actually illuminated why what had happened to me had happened. I guess, in the end, that hardly mattered. I was just glad it had happened at all.

We never encountered another human being like me.

And as time went on, the happenings of my appearance here felt more like a dream than some miracle. It was more like I had always been here, next to Apollo. He had the river on one side. Meanwhile, I, River, was standing next to him on the other side.

Was this my purpose?

I wasn't sure.

But maybe my purpose was nothing more than to achieve my own happiness.

And as I interlaced my fingers with Apollo's, I knew this was something I could only do with this being by my side.

PART SIX

APOLLO

CHAPTER ELEVEN

Before River

Alone.

Yes, I had always been alone, and I knew nothing else.

My only company was the glowing souls that traveled at night and slept during the day. My existence was relatively empty, except for the few times I could feel the souls calling for me. It wasn't often, but on the occasional night, as I walked, I could feel something burning within the antlers on my head.

The tines would react in specific directions, drawing me to the place where the stranded soul would be.

There, I'd find the souls waiting for me.

Their lights would flicker and shine, as if they were calling to me, but without a sound.

They were so small and precious, completely counter to how dense and determined they were. No matter how long it took them, no matter how many times they ended up on the shore, these little souls were determined to make it to where they belonged.

It was hard not to root for them, which was why, as I picked them up to get them back on their way, I would whisper kind words to spur them on.

And so night after night went.

During the day, though I couldn't see the souls, I could still sense they were there, and that gave me a minute amount of comfort. Still, the days were long, and as I wandered along the shore, awaiting the night, my mind was hopelessly empty.

But then I felt it.

There was the familiar burning in one of my tines.

Well, it began in one of my tines. But steadily, it spread from one tine to the next until both of my antlers were positively burning as a soul screamed for me. It was an intensity I had never experienced before, especially during the daytime.

My head was pounding, but as I turned around to look for the soul, what I found was not any soul I had seen before.

It was a whole human whose soul burned so brightly that it entirely encapsulated their form as they appeared in the middle of the river. I could hardly believe my eyes. It was a bright, golden light blooming from the middle of the river. It was so intense I had to look away, but I found myself unable to look away entirely.

Something was coming that wasn't just calling me. My entire body was shivering with the intensity of how desperately this soul and I were being drawn to one another. It was as if a piece of me was manifesting outside of my body, and I needed to retrieve it.

Finally, the light went out, and what I found in its place was a form, not unlike my own. I was aware that souls were the cores of humans, but I had never seen a human before. Discovering that I might not have been so different from humans themselves was comforting in some way.

I was just beginning to make my way toward the form when they suddenly erupted with movement. Souls moved, but not like this, and seeing the violence of it left me stunned. Their limbs flailed, sending water flying through the air. My tines reacted as souls that couldn't be seen were probably being flung about by the human's movements.

I wanted to call out to the human, hopefully, to calm them, but then they began to make the most frightening sound. It was a high-pitched wail that cut through the silence with a sharpness that shook me to my core. I dropped to the ground, covering my ears, though that did little to stop the terrible sound from coming through.

They continued to flail and flail, eventually working themselves up until they were sitting up out of the water. Their hair was sticking to the sides of their face, their forehead, and along the sides of their neck. Their eyes were wide, their mouth wide open as they took in gasping breaths.

Our eyes met.

Even in his panicked state, I couldn't help thinking he was beautiful.

I straightened up, trying to come up with something to say so I wouldn't scare him, though the words were gumming up in my throat. This was the first conscience soul I had ever encountered, and I really wanted to appear as wise and dependable as possible.

But by the time I made it into the water and was hovering above him, I didn't have a single word prepared. Staring down at the soaked human, shaking in the river's waters, the only thing I could think to say was the most obvious:

"You aren't supposed to be here."

He blinked.

"Yeah."

It was the first time in my life that I had said something and received a response, and it was such an innocent reaction that I had to force myself not to smile. But then his arms wrapped around himself, and he began to shake. My heart lurched.

"You are cold. Let me help you."

I held out my hand and was surprised at how easily he reciprocated. I was almost as surprised by how large his hands were. He appeared so small to me, but he was more like me than I had expected. I could see that much more clearly now with the sharp line of his jaw and the Adam's apple bobbing at the front of his neck.

Yet, lifting him was easy. His body seemed to float right out of the water and then crumpled against mine. The water that had soaked into his clothes, which clung to his skin, was steadily soaking into me. It was chilly, but my eternal heat was easily drying it away.

I was just about to guide the human safely to shore when his body twitched, threatening to tense up as his hands formed fists in the folds of my cloak. Ducking my head to check his face, I found him frowning, his eyelids flickering as he furiously fought against sleep. It reminded me a bit of the flickering of the souls just before daybreak when they took their rest.

Quietly, I whispered:

"Go to sleep. The next time you wake up, you'll be somewhere safer."

I half expected him to disappear as his eyes slid shut, but he didn't. As his body fully slumped against mine, he remained right where he was and where I could see him. I couldn't explain why, but it made my heart flutter in my chest.

As I lifted him into my arms, I was stunned by how cool he was. Souls were warm at all times, and I had always assumed the beings they came from were the same. But as I cradled this human's limp body against me and felt his chill begin to warm and match my own temperature, I realized then this was what life was. This was what made souls alive.

They changed.

I wasn't quite sure what purpose this soul had, but for the first time in my entire existence, I looked forward to what might be different when he woke up.

Thank you so much for reading.
For future projects and updates, check out my
website:
kitshaw.com

If you'd like spicy, open-door extras, check out my
Patreon:
patreon.com/KitShaw